# DON'T GO NEAR THE WATER!

Veronika Martenova Charles

Illustrated by David Parkins

Tundra Books

Published in Canada by Tundra Books,
75 Sherbourne Street, Toronto, Ontario M5A 2P9

Published in the United States by Tundra Books of Northern New York,
P.O. Box 1030, Plattsburgh, New York 12901

Library of Congress Control Number: 2006903147

**Library and Archives Canada Cataloguing in Publication**

Charles, Veronika Martenova
    Don't go near the water! / Veronika Martenova Charles ; [illustrated by]
David Parkins.

(Easy-to-read spooky tales)
ISBN 978–0–88776–780–7

    1. Horror tales, Canadian (English). 2. Children's stories, Canadian
(English). I. Parkins, David II. Charles, Veronika Martenova. Easy-to-read
spooky tales. III. Title.

PS8555.H42242D59 2007        jC813'.54        C2006–901940–1

ONTARIO ARTS COUNCIL
CONSEIL DES ARTS DE L'ONTARIO

We acknowledge the financial support of the Government of Canada through the Book
Publishing Industry Development Program (BPIDP) and that of the Government of
Ontario through the Ontario Media Development Corporation's Ontario Book Initiative.
We further acknowledge the support of the Canada Council for the Arts and the Ontario
Arts Council for our publishing program.

Printed and bound in Canada

1  2  3  4  5  6        12  11  10  09  08  07

# CONTENTS

# THE CREEK
## PART I

On Monday, it rained.

Tuesday, it poured.

By Wednesday, the rain stopped

and the sun came out.

"Let's go for a walk,"

I said to Marcos after school.

We went to Leon's house

and rang his doorbell.

"Can Leon come out and play?"

we asked his mother.

"Yes," she said,

"but don't go near the water!

The creek is high after the rain."

We walked to the park

and looked at the creek

from the path.

"Look at all the foam in the water!

It's like there is soap in it,"

I said.

"Maybe it's the water people

blowing bubbles," Marcos said.

"I'll tell you a story if you want."

"About the water people?"

asked Leon.

"Yes, and about a quarry," said Marcos.

"What's a quarry?" I asked.

"It's a huge hole in the ground,

where people have dug out rocks,"

explained Marcos.

"So tell us the story," I said.

# CHILDREN WITH GREEN TEETH

## (Marcos' Story)

Henry could take the road

to school,

or he could take a shortcut

past the quarry.

The quarry was filled with water,

and people said that long ago,

two children had drowned there.

Now their ghosts

haunted the place.

One day, Henry was late

for school.

"I'll take the shortcut,"

he told his mother.

"Be careful," she said.

"And don't go near the water!"

Henry hurried off,

but slowed down

as he passed the quarry.

There was a bad smell in the air.

What was down there?

Henry walked to the edge

of the quarry.

The water was bubbling.

Was it hot? Henry leaned over

and stuck his hand in.

Something grabbed him!

Four slimy green arms

pulled him underwater,

and pushed him

through a hole

and up onto a ledge in a cave.

In the dim light, Henry saw

two skinny green children

with big green teeth.

"We've been here for a long time

and we are bored," they said.

"You have to play with us

or we will eat you!"

The children threw something.

"Catch our ball,"

they ordered.

It was a skull!

Henry was scared.

He thought fast.

"I have a better idea," he said.

"Let's play hide and seek.

Close your eyes and count

to sixty, while I hide."

The children covered their eyes

and started counting.

*"One, two, three . . ."*

Henry looked around.

*"Ten, eleven, twelve . . ."*

He had to find the opening.

*"Twenty, twenty-one . . ."*

Where was it?

There!

Behind a pile of bones was a hole.

It had to be the way out.

Henry squeezed through it

and disappeared.

*"Thirty, thirty-one . . ."*

Henry was in the tunnel,

and could see a gate

ahead of him.

He pushed it open

and dived into the water.

He saw light and swam toward it.

But two dark shapes

were coming after him.

Their mouths were open,

their long teeth ready to strike.

Four slimy green arms

reached for him. . . .

18

They were fast,

but Henry was so scared,

he was faster.

He burst out of the water

and ran all the way home.

And after that, Henry *never*

went near that water again.

"I know a story about

water people, too," I said.

"Okay, but so do I," said Leon.

"Can I tell mine first?

It's about the ocean."

# DEADLY BEACH

(Leon's Story)

There was only one beach

on the island.

It had white sand and clear water.

It was a beautiful,

but deadly place.

Sometimes people who swam

there didn't come back.

When Kai and Lana went out,

their father would always say,

"Don't go near the water!"

But sometimes it was hot,

and Kai and Lana would go to

the beach with their friends.

To get there, they had to pass

by Makani's house.

Makani was a strange man.

He had a hump on his back

and wore a cape to hide it.

Whenever people passed by,

he would ask,

"Are you going to the beach?"

Then Makani would point

to someone and say,

"You, with no legs,

enjoy your swim!"

Later, that person would

float ashore . . . with no legs.

One day Lana asked,

"How can Makani tell

what will happen?"

"I don't know," Kai answered.

"And why does he wear

that cape? He's strange.

Let's spy on him."

They hid near Makani's house.

When he came out,

Kai and Lana followed him.

They saw Makani climb into

a lava tube that led

to the ocean.

Kai and Lana peered in,

but they didn't see Makani.

They went inside.

"Look! There's his cape!"

said Lana. "He must have gone

for a swim."

Suddenly Makani was back.

He stood there dripping,

and then he bent down

to get his cape.

"Ahhh!" Kai and Lana screamed.

Sticking out of Makani's back,

were the jaws of a shark!

"SHARKMAN!" they cried.

The Sharkman looked up

and saw the two children.

He chased them,

but he was too slow,

and they made it home.

Now they knew why

their father always said,

"Don't go near the water!"

★  ★  ★

"So he could still be

out there, right?" Marcos asked.

He looked a little scared.

"He is a shark, so he can

only be in the ocean," I said.

"No," said Leon.

"He is a shark*man.*

He can go anywhere he wants.

He could even be in this creek!"

"Oh, you're silly," I told him.

"Now it's time for my story.

It's about the Waterman."

## WATERMAN

(My Story)

Marie and her mother

lived in a house by the river.

Every day Marie went to

the water to wash their clothes.

One morning, Mother said,

"Last night I had a bad dream.

I saw you all wet

and covered with fish scales.

Don't go near the water, Marie!"

"Oh, Mother!" Marie sighed.

"It was only a dream."

And she went to wash

their clothes.

She put her blouse into the river.

*SPLASH!*

The water exploded beside her.

A Waterman burst out of

the water and grabbed Marie.

He dragged her

to the bottom of the river

and into his house.

There were puddles on the floors

and green slime on the walls.

"I've been watching you,"

the Waterman said.

"You're good at cleaning.

From now on,

you will clean my house."

Marie had no choice.

She washed slime off the walls

and sang to keep from crying.

"*La, la, la, la.*"

"Stop that!" said the Waterman.

"I can't stand your singing."

"I can't stop," said Marie.

"I sing because I'm sad.

I didn't get to say good-bye

to my mother.

*La, la, la,*" she began

to sing again.

"I would turn you into a fish,

but then you couldn't

clean my house,"

the Waterman said.

"Promise to return by sundown,

and you can go to say good-bye."

"I promise, I promise!" said Marie.

So the Waterman took her up

to the riverbank.

Marie's mother was happy

to see her daughter again.

"You're not going back,"

she told Marie.

"But I have to keep my promise,"

Marie cried.

"Don't worry, you're safe now,"

said Mother.

And she locked the door.

At sundown, they heard footsteps.

*Bang! Bang!*

Someone was knocking

on the door.

"Time to go, Marie!"

It was the Waterman.

"You can't have her!"

cried Mother.

*BANG! BANG! BANG!*

The Waterman was angry.

"Come out, Marie!

You promised," he called.

"Go jump in the river!"

Mother shouted.

"Leave my daughter alone!"

It was quiet outside.

Then Mother heard

footsteps leaving.

45

"He's gone, Marie!

Everything is all right now,"

Mother said, as she went

back to the kitchen.

"Marie?" There was no answer.

Marie wasn't there.

But on the kitchen floor,

flopping in a puddle of water

was a fish.

It had a face.

It looked like Marie. . . .

★  ★  ★

# THE CREEK
## PART 2

"Look!" Leon shouted.

"There's a fish beside the creek.

I'm going to take a look.

Maybe it's Marie."

He got up and walked

toward the creek.

"Come back!" I called.

"Don't go near the water!

It's slippery there."

"No, it's not," Leon called back –

and he slid on the mud.

*SPLASH!*

Leon was in the water!

We ran to the creek.

"Help!" Leon screamed.

I yelled to Marcos,

"Quick! Get a stick!"

Marcos found a branch

and we held it out to Leon.

He grabbed the branch

and we dragged him

out of the creek.

"Ahhh!" Leon cried.

Something green and slimy

was stuck to his leg!

"It's the children with green teeth!"

We pulled him free and ran.

We reached Leon's house.

"I'm freezing," he shivered.

"My mom makes me

take a hot bath when I'm cold,"

I said. "Try it. It will warm you up."

"No way," said Leon.

"I've had enough!

I'm never going near water again!"

# AFTERWORD

At the end of *Waterman,*

Marie has just been turned into

a fish. But what happens next?

Is there a way for Marie

and her mother to break the spell?

Will Marie be a fish forever?

What will her life be like then?

# WHERE THE STORIES COME FROM

The characters in *Children with Green Teeth* were inspired by an English water spirit called Jenny Greenteeth. *Deadly Beach* is based on a Hawaiian legend. Characters like the Waterman are often found in the folktales of Central Europe. In the past, such stories may have been invented to frighten children away from unsafe water.